EVANGELIST OF LIGHT

ROBERT DALE

Scripture quotations marked KJV are taken from the Holy Bible, King James Version, which is in the public domain.

This is a work of fiction. Names, characters, places and incidents either are the product of the author's imagination or are used fictitiously, and any resemblance to actual persons, living or dead, businesses, companies, events, or locales is entirely coincidental.

ISBN: 978-1-4866-2696-0
eBook ISBN: 978-1-4866-2697-7

Word Alive Press
119 De Baets Street Winnipeg, MB R2J 3R9
www.wordalivepress.ca

WORD ALIVE
—P R E S S—

Cataloguing in Publication information can be obtained from Library and Archives Canada.

To Mom and Dad:
Thank you for your support,
encouragement, and assistance. I love you both.

"And he said unto them, Go ye into all the world, and preach the gospel to every creature" (Mark 16:15).

After this I beheld, and, lo, a great multitude, which no man could number, of all nations, and kindreds, and people, and tongues, stood before the throne, and before the Lamb, clothed with white robes, and palms in their hands; And cried with a loud voice, saying, Salvation to our God which sitteth upon the throne, and unto the Lamb. (Revelation 7:9–10)

Oﬆ

"Welcome to the family!"

These were the first words he heard after accepting Jesus as his Lord and Saviour.

The first thing he saw, however, was what appeared to be three ancient soldiers standing before him. They were dressed in full armour, almost like Roman soldiers of old, which glowed with an unusual light.

"You all are warriors of God!" he exclaimed in rapt wonder.

"So are you now," the one man replied while extending a hand to lift him from the ground. He had fallen to his knees as he'd cried out his need for Jesus.

"My name's Dave," the man added as he assisted him to his feet.

"Kathy." The next extended hand came from a woman, which startled him.

"Women can be soldiers of God?" he asked in surprise.

"Yes, everyone is invited to become followers of Jesus, and we all have a role in the army of God."

Just then, the only familiar person out of these three warriors extended a coffee towards him.

"Hey, Kranti, have a coffee. It will help you focus." This was Ben, a coworker of his and the main reason he had come to this place.

He accepted the coffee as they walked to the pickup parked nearby. Ben opened the tailgate for them to sit on. As Kranti sipped on his coffee, his focus suddenly switched to how he'd seen the world before he had prayed. He now saw three ordinary looking people before him dressed in normal clothing.

"What happened? You all look normal now, not like warriors anymore!"

A light chuckle from the three of them almost made him angry until Ben said, "You'll get used to that. We can switch between viewing the world around us in the spiritual realm and viewing it in the physical realm. Food helps bring our focus back to the physical."

Kranti nodded as though he understood. He did not.

"I know you have a lot of questions. We did as well when we first got saved," Dave said.

"Saved? What does this mean?" Kranti asked in a concerned and confused tone.

"It's what we call those who have accepted Jesus. The Bible often talks about being saved," Kathy put in.

"Oh."

"Here, this one is yours. I suggest starting at the book of John." Dave handed him a brand-new black Bible.

"Really? For me? How much?"

"No cost; it's free."

He looked at Dave's face and could see the man meant it. Kranti tried to hand the book back. "I don't read English too good."

"Take it for now. You need to start studying God's Word so you can learn more about Jesus and grow spiritually."

He wanted to learn more about Jesus, so he took the book begrudgingly and muttered a half-hearted, "Thank you."

"I'll get you one in your own language," Ben offered. "Then maybe you can understand the Word of God better."

This sounded great to Kranti, but he was so used to hiding his true feelings from others that he simply said, "Okay."

"We need to get out of here. Our permit time is running out," Dave reminded Ben.

"Oh yeah. Okay, Kranti, I think we should continue to talk. There's a lot you're trying to understand right now, yes?"

The new believer nodded. He really did want to understand what had happened to him.

Kranti agreed to meet with Ben at Murphy's so they could talk some more, and the two men set out towards the truck-stop.

Unbeknownst to the two men, the dark beings had begun to watch from a distance.

Two

ranti called a cab to meet with Ben, and during the ride he was beginning to feel silly. Had he actually seen these warriors? He'd been quite drunk, after all, though he didn't feel drunk at all now.

Unseen black, smoky shadows were collecting around the back of the taxi.

Kranti was just about to tell the driver to take him back home instead when he felt a comforting warmth in his chest and a clarity in his mind. He didn't know what to think of this, but he suddenly knew he wanted to talk with Ben about Jesus, so they continued towards the truck stop.

In the spiritual realm, a glow had resonated from within Kranti, and this caused the shadows that were following to retreat.

He flipped open the Bible Dave had given him to see a verse he had never heard before. "*If the Son therefore shall make you free, ye shall be free indeed*," (John 8:36).

Son?

Whose Son?

Free from what?

Even as he asked these questions within his own mind, he felt that he knew the answers to them.

Jesus.

God's Son.

Free from himself, his old habits and patterns, from the self-destruction he'd always known.

He felt that he wanted to pray, but he wasn't certain how. He had only done it once before, and the others had been there to guide him the first time. He decided to make an attempt.

Hello. Jesus? He prayed in his thoughts because to do so aloud would be too embarrassing. *I don't really know what's happening in me right now, and I don't really know how to talk to you. But I need to know if all of this is real or if I'm still drunk and imagining it all.* He stopped there and waited, not knowing what he was waiting for.

The Bible in his hands was still open. A page flipped over, so he looked down at it. Part of a verse seemed to almost jump off of the page at him: "… *him that cometh to me I will in no wise cast out*" (John 6:37b). Even with his less than perfect English, he knew what this was saying.

"Thank you, Lord Jesus, I hear you."

He didn't know why, but tears of joy were running down his face, and he quickly wiped them away as they pulled into the cafe.

THREE

Kranti saw Ben's truck parked at the far end of the row of parking stalls. Ben was leaning against the truck; he had two coffees on the hood. Passing one to Kranti, he flopped the tailgate down and sat on it, inviting the second man to join him.

"Hey, glad you didn't change your mind. This is too much coffee for me."

He laughed at his own joke. Kranti hopped up on the tailgate, looking at Ben suspiciously. "I almost went home. How did you know?"

"You're human, just like me. We all have our doubts, especially when we first trust Jesus."

Kranti thought about this and could see the truth in what Ben had said. Taking the coffee, he thanked Ben and then told him of his experience on the way over.

"I had something happen in the taxi that I don't understand."

"Okay, what happened?" A look of curiosity showed on Ben's face.

"I felt like this stuff was just from me being drunk. That's when I almost told the driver to take me home. But then I felt warm inside my chest"—he touched his chest with an open hand to emphasize the point—"and suddenly my thoughts were clear and I knew I wanted to talk to you about this. Then I opened the Bible and read some things that sounded like Jesus was talking to me."

A smile from Ben told him he understood.

"It was Him," Ben said. "I've experienced that myself many times since becoming a Christian. What did you read? Can you find the verses again?"

"I don't think so, but it talked about the Son and being free and Him not casting me out."

Ben recognized the scripture and quickly found it in the Bible that Kranti still carried. He explained the verses, and Kranti confirmed that he had felt and thought exactly how Ben said it.

"Okay, so you see that the Holy Spirit is helping you to understand what you read."

"The Holy Spirit? You mean like Father, Son, and Holy Spirit?"

"Yes, I'm surprised you know that phrase."

"There was a Catholic church close to where I grew up. I read it on their sign many times."

Ben nodded. "I see. Yes, this is the person I'm talking about."

"He's real too? Just like Jesus?"

"Yes, very much. That's how the Holy Trinity works. God the Father is one person. God the Son, Jesus, is another person, and God the Holy Spirit is the third person who make up the Trinity."

Kranti didn't understand, but he felt that warm comfort in his chest again and had a peace in his mind about these things. He decided to trust what Ben was saying as true.

"How do I switch into seeing the spiritual stuff?"

"I usually just think about the Lord and it switches on its own."

"Okay, I'll try."

Kranti focused on what he thought Jesus looked like. Suddenly, the world around him changed! He was seeing different forms of darkness and light passing by each other, usually connected to a person, and when he saw his own reflection in the window, he was amazed. "Wow, I *am* a warrior of God!"

FOUR

The joy on Kranti's face was completely different from the man's usual grumpy scowl. It was clear that he had found peace and joy through Christ! As he examined the other warrior in front of him, he noticed some things that were different from his own look.

"How come my cloak is a different colour than yours?" he asked.

"The colour tells us what your position is in the army of God. I'm a warrior of light, which is why mine is red. Your colour tells me that you're an evangelist of God, because it's silver."

"What does evangelist mean?"

"It means someone who spreads the news of salvation to many others."

"I feel comforted and powerful towards this idea, but I'm also scared. Who am I supposed to tell about Jesus?"

"I think maybe the people here who came from your own country. Maybe start with your own family."

A look of trepidation came over Kranti's face as he considered this.

"My culture would be against the idea that Jesus is God's Son. They think of Him as a prophet, nothing more."

"You'd be surprised how many people from your country are turning to Jesus. We have a small group that holds their own church service in a separate auditorium at Harmony Church, where I attend."

This did surprise Kranti, and it showed. "Really? How many of my countrymen are there?"

"I'd guess about twenty or so, maybe even thirty."

"I'd like to meet them."

At that moment, two figures rode into the parking lot on motorcycles and veered towards them. Sammy and another biker rolled along on their choppers, and Kranti could see they weren't alone.

Dark beings were floating in the air behind them, riding on the bikes with them, and even clinging to their backs!

Five

S ammy and his compatriot rumbled into the spots next to Ben's pickup, leaned the large machines over onto their stands, and hit the kill switches. As they dismounted the choppers, Sammy strode towards his co-workers, with his riding partner and the shadowy figures in tow.

"Since when did you two hang out?" This snide comment showed the direction in which this conversation would go. Ben came to Kranti's defence.

"We've settled our differences. And since when is it your business what we do?" Ben knew from his spiritual perspective that this wasn't his best argument. The demonic presence was united in making mocking gestures towards the two warriors.

"After all of the complaints I've heard from you about Kranti? Come on, what are you trying to pull?" Sammy then spied the Bible in Kranti's hands. "Really? You think this heathen can actually find God?"

In the spiritual realm, the largest demon made an advance, swinging a large battle axe. To Ben's surprise, Kranti stepped forward, raising his shield and stating, "… *him that cometh to me I will in no wise cast out*." Blocking the blow as he quoted the scripture, his sword also came up, piercing the chest of the demon and disposing of the enemy! The lesser demons backed off in fear and surprise.

"Okay, okay, I was just joking!" Sammy pulled back from his attack. "Are you actually a Christian now?" The question seemed genuine.

"Yes, I have just become a Christian." Kranti looked radiant as he confessed his new-found faith. In the spiritual realm, he emitted a powerful glow as he made his announcement. Ben hadn't experienced this type of spiritual capability and wanted to discuss this with Kranti.

Sammy and the demonic horde with him both took a step back at Kranti's statement. The other biker gave Sammy a look.

"Um, okay then, well, we need to eat. Catch you guys at work."

It was a quick retreat, and Ben for one was glad that the battle was over. Kranti, however, was excited and seemed eager for more battle.

"Wow, that was a demon! I just fought with a demon!" The new Christian was overjoyed at defeating his enemy.

"Yes, it was. How did you know how to fight it? I needed some training to know to quote scripture while fighting them."

"I don't know how. I just knew it was right to say what Jesus had said to me."

"That seems to fit, but what about the glowing from your chest? I've never seen that!" The "senior" Christian looked confused.

"How should I know? I became a Christian one hour ago. All I know is it felt like when I was comforted in the taxi."

"I think we need to talk to Arpit about these things. He's the leader of the small church at Harmony."

Kranti felt this was a good idea, but he also knew it was getting late, so he decided to go home and wait for Arpit's call.

As the two men parted ways, the dark beings watched.

Six

Kranti pulled into his parking space at his home and thought about what he would say to Saachi, his wife. He knew she wouldn't really have a problem with him showing respect to Jesus. It was a part of the Hindu beliefs that Jesus was a highly learned man, or a man who cast off traditional life. He was sometimes even thought of as a deity descended to earth. He knew that she would disagree with Jesus being the only way to God. He had never been more afraid to face her, even when he'd lost a large amount of money gambling.

Praying seemed to be the only right choice.

"Lord Jesus, I want so much to tell Saachi about you, but you know how much she believes in the Hindu way. I ask for your help, please, with how to tell her about what I've found in you. In Jesus' name. Amen."

He suddenly felt again that now-familiar warmth in his chest and heard a voice saying, "My grace is sufficient for thee." This was something he had seen on one of those Catholic church signs, but he knew it was from the Lord.

"Okay, thank you, Lord." With this, he got out of his car and went inside the house.

Saachi was in the kitchen finishing up cleaning and preparing for the coming day. Kranti walked in, and she glanced his way with a disapproving look. She then got a confused expression on her face and examined him more closely.

"You seem different." She came closer and took a sniff. "Why are you not drunk?" It was actually said in an accusing tone, even though it was against Hindu practices to drink alcohol.

"Something happened to me tonight, something that changed my life."

"What, did you go to the temple for once?" A mocking tone again.

"No, this is real, the most real thing I've ever experienced."

A concerned look crossed his wife's face. " W h a t ? Did you meet some whore?" She knew he had never done this but couldn't hold back her frustration.

"I met someone else. I met Jesus Christ. I'm a Christian now." He waited with bated breath, not expecting a good response.

She paused, and he could see her calculating what this meant.

"Do you mean that you have abandoned Hinduism?"

This was it. That dreaded moment of truth.

"I mean I have found the true way to God."

"There are many paths to God. If you have found one that finally works for you, I am happy. Maybe you will finally stop drinking and gambling."

It was a shot at him, he knew, but maybe she'd see the power of Jesus in him, he hoped.

"Well, I'm finished here and I'm going to bed." She gave him one last look. "We'll talk more about this tomorrow." He nodded his assent and watched her head off towards bed.

Dark beings were watching and growing unhappy.

Seven

Kranti woke up feeling better than he had in years. He knew it had to be because of the weight that had been lifted off his shoulders after becoming a Christian. He felt free of past burdens and worries, doubts and fears, and it was wonderful.

He got dressed and headed downstairs for coffee. Saachi was already in the kitchen making breakfast at the stove when he walked in.

He stepped up behind her, wrapped his arms around her waist, and gave her a kiss on the cheek.

"Good morning," he said.

"I'm cooking, be careful!" She gave him a sideways glare. "What's wrong with you?"

"I just feel good and I love you. What's wrong with that?" He felt annoyed at her annoyance.

"You haven't kissed me just to say you love me in a very long time. What's changed?"

She obviously wasn't connecting his mood to his new-found faith.

"I feel different this morning," he replied, the mood quickly shifting. "Why is that bad?"

If Kranti had been viewing the spiritual realm, he would have seen the dark beings laughing around the kitchen. Instead, he poured himself a coffee and sat at the table, deciding to read from his new Bible.

Just as he began to read, the sound of his sons coming down the stairs distracted him.

"Rachit! Talat!" Saachi called to the boys. "Don't run down the stairs!"

When she noticed Kranti reading at the kitchen table, she pointed a finger at him.

"No, I don't want you influencing them with that Bible," she said. "Read that somewhere else!"

Because he'd been focused on the Word of God, he was in the spiritual realm when he lifted his head to his wife. Suddenly he noticed all the dark beings surrounding his wife. One was even whispering in her ear!

"Saachi, please let me try to explain to you and the boys what has happened to me," he pleaded.

He desperately wanted to chase these demons away from his family and home, but she was unwavering in her stance.

"No, we have our gods and you can't tell us to change who we worship," she insisted. "Now take that book out of here. I don't want it in my house!"

He poured his coffee into his travel mug, picked up his Bible, and headed out the door. As he left, the demons in his home were delirious.

Eight

S itting in his car in the driveway, Kranti felt unsure of what to do. His wife had kicked him out before, but never for this reason. He normally would go to a bar, but he no longer felt the urge to do that, especially first thing in the morning. He sensed that he should pray, so he began.

"Lord Jesus, I don't know what to do at this point, so I'm coming to you," he began. "Please direct me, Lord. In your name I pray. Amen."

As he opened his eyes, he noticed the card that Ben had given him with Arpit's name and number.

"Thank you, Lord," he whispered.

He dialled the number on the card and waited.

"Arpit Brar speaking," said the voice on the other end of the line.

"Hello, Arpit. My name is Kranti Kholi. Ben Parsons gave me your number."

"Oh yes. Ben mentioned you might call me. How can I help?"

"I would like to speak with you about Jesus," Kranti said. "I just became a Christian."

"Okay. We have a Bible study starting in an hour. Why don't you come over and we can chat after?"

Since Kranti had nowhere else to go, he agreed to attend. But first he decided to drive over to Murphy's and get some breakfast.

As he pulled into the truck stop, he noticed many motorcycles parked in a row. One of them stood out from the others; it was painted orange with silver flames and had obviously been made for a large rider.

Sammy.

Kranti said a quick prayer. Feeling peace, he walked into the diner. Just as the motorcycles had been lined up outside, he found a row of bikers lined up along the counter. They were eating and being loud. It seemed obvious to him that they felt this was their place.

He chose a booth away from the clamour and sat down.

Suddenly, a loud voice boomed across the restaurant.

"Well, look what we have here! You think you can come in here whenever you want, Hindu?"

Kranti quickly recognized that the man was talking to him. He turned around to see Sammy and the other bikers looking his way.

"This is a public restaurant," Kranti replied. "Anyone can come here."

"This place is ours." Sammy was putting on a display of bravado, the likes of which Kranti had never seen. "We own it and we don't want you here."

The old anger began to build up in him.

"You don't own it," he retorted. "It belongs to Murphy, and you know it!"

He was too smart to think it was going to end with that, but he couldn't think of anything else to say.

The antagonists rose from their stools at the counter and approached Kranti in a menacing fashion. As they advanced, Kranti said a quick prayer, which shifted him back into the spiritual realm. What he saw terrified him. The biker group was surrounded by a gathering of demons even larger than the group itself!

Kranti watched in amazement as a group of men, spiritual soldiers, rose up from the nearby tables and approached the bikers, telling them to stop and leave the man alone. But the bikers didn't listen, nor did the demonic horde egging them on.

A sudden flash of blinding light illuminated the diner, and five bright figures suddenly landed in the midst of the escalating conflict.

Angels!

At the sight of the angelic force, the demons shrank back. The bikers began to back off as well. They looked to a long, red-haired biker, who motioned for them to leave, just as the sound of police sirens reached Kranti's ears.

The angels vanished after the threat was gone.

Kranti could not have been more surprised by this turn of events. He sank into his seat as the rumble of motorbikes faded into the distance.

Πίπε

The five old soldiers came to the booth where Kranti was sitting and introduced themselves. Kranti told them his name and explained that he had just become a believer in Jesus. He thanked them for their help.

"Good to meet you, Kranti. We could see that they were going to do something very bad. Those bikers have a reputation in Dalberton."

"Who are they?"

"They call themselves Red's Riders; they've been around here for decades," another of the men explained.

"I know one of them from my workplace. We've never gotten along."

"The big one who spoke?"

"Yes, that's the guy. Sammy."

"We'll pray about this for you. We're just getting ready for a prayer meeting at Harmony Christian Fellowship

Church. Would you like to come along?" a third man asked.

"I'm supposed to be meeting a man there named Arpit."

"Yes, that's who we're meeting with."

Kranti agreed to follow the men there later, and they let him eat in peace.

He finished his meal and headed to the church. As he walked up to the front door of the church, he was impressed with the size of the building. It was elegant in a Western fashion and large enough to rival some of the larger Hindu temples.

He entered the building and was immediately at peace and even felt joy within his chest. He looked around and saw many Western men but also many from his own country. This was obviously a meeting of both church groups, and he felt both at ease and a little nervous. Taking his place in a pew, he watched, not knowing what to expect, as a man walked up to the front and addressed them.

"Welcome to all, and thank you for coming to this prayer meeting. If you're new here, we are happy to see you. Don't feel like you have to take part in the prayers. It's okay to just watch and pray in silence. Now, who would like to start?"

One of the men Kranti saw at the restaurant stood up and prayed aloud.

"Lord, thank you that we can meet like this and bring to you the concerns we have for ourselves and others. We bring before you this man we met this morning at Murphy's and the ones who were troubling him. Lord, please continue to keep Kranti from harm and from Satan's destructive efforts in his life. We also pray for these bikers and this man Sammy. We ask, Lord Jesus, that you will speak to them, and Sammy specifically, so that they find you and are saved. In Jesus' name. Amen."

Kranti was humbled to the point of tears. As he wept silently, he thanked the Lord in prayer.

Many men stood where they were and prayed aloud. The prayers were heartfelt and resonated much care and compassion for those being mentioned. What surprised Kranti was that none of the prayers seemed to be preset like many in the Hindu faith; the men just prayed from their hearts. The service lasted for an hour. At the end, the same man who had opened it stood up front again.

"Thank you for those very compassionate prayers. As usual, we have coffee and donuts, so please stick around and chat with us, if you like."

Kranti stood up and began to look around, as other men were doing the same. One man seemed most likely to be Arpit, as he had several men talking with him. Kranti made his way towards him.

Just as Kranti drew near to the group, a man turned and froze in place, as did Kranti. Both men stood facing each other in surprise, with fear etched on their faces.

Zavian Shah, a level 2 supervisor from the warehouse, stood before him.

Ten

As the two men stood facing each other, Arpit turned from his previous conversation and addressed Kranti.

"You must be Kranti. I'm Arpit. I'm glad you made it." He offered his hand in greeting, and Kranti shook it.

"Yes, thank you." The tension between Zavian and Kranti was obvious, so Arpit addressed it.

"Do you two know each other?"

"Yes, we work together." Zavian spoke first, and Kranti offered a quiet assent.

"Oh, I had no idea. Well, let's get some coffee and talk, shall we?"

They all wandered over to the tables that were set with coffee dispensers and boxes of donuts. After they mixed their preferred drinks, they found an empty table, sat down, and began the task of understanding one another.

"I didn't expect to see you here," Kranti said to Zavian.

"It was quite a shock for me as well. Have you become a Christian?"

"Yes, just last night I accepted Jesus as my own Lord and Saviour."

"Praise God! That's awesome! I've been a Christian for a few months now myself."

"You kept this to yourself at the warehouse," Kranti stated.

"Yes. With so many others from our country working there, I'm afraid of what might be said or done."

Kranti understood this. Many Hindu people get very angry when one of their own chooses to follow Jesus.

"My own wife just this morning told me to take my Bible out of our house," Kranti shared.

Arpit stepped into the conversation by making a suggestion.

"You both are new enough believers that I think a little guidance on the spiritual side of life would be good."

Both men agreed.

"Okay, let's shift into the spiritual view and examine some things."

All three of them focused, and after shifting their views, took a look around the auditorium. They saw not only themselves but also the rest of the attendees dressed in full armour. It felt like being transported back two thousand years to a Roman centurion camp! The soldiers were all wearing full armour sets, including shields, and each had an exquisite sword strapped to their side. Kranti noticed, however, that the shields weren't all the same size and that each man's cloak varied in colour.

Arpit got the two men's attention by clearing his throat.

"You see how different things are when viewing the spiritual side of life?"

"Why are the shields different sizes? Is that because of our position within the army of God?" Zavian asked.

"No, that's shown by your cloak colour, but we'll get into that next. The shield size differences reflect the individuals' growth in faith in Jesus Christ."

"What is faith?" Kranti asked.

"Trust is the most basic answer to that, but it becomes much more as we grow in our faith in Jesus."

The two young Christians looked at their own shields, noting their similar size. They then examined the other shields around the room, noting that most of the largest shields belonged to the oldest men. This made things easier to understand for Kranti, as he compared the growth in faith to physical growth.

"The other thing I'd like to explain is the difference in colour of the cloaks. Mine is purple with some silver, while

Zavian's is a deep blue sapphire. Kranti, yours is brilliant silver."

They looked at each other's cloaks.

"I'll start with mine. The purple is for priesthood, which is what the leaders of churches and speakers will mostly have. Now we get into the silver on mine, which means the same thing as Kranti's cloak. Silver is for evangelists, those who spread God's Word amongst many people. Sapphire is given to those with a gift of divine revelation, insight into things that the Lord wants them to know or that the enemy is trying to conceal. There are many other colours and positions. Okay, let's shift back into the physical view. Have a doughnut; it helps."

Eleven

Arpit had given them a lot to think about. He had explained that each soldier in the army of God had different abilities, and that Kranti's was basically to emit a very bright light from within himself when in times of danger. He also explained that it would drive away the darkness and demons whenever he let it shine. It was a lot to take in.

Walking into the kitchen at home, Kranti could tell that Saachi wasn't happy. She turned to face him, and he could see the stony set of her face. This was serious.

"Where have you been? You've been gone for hours."

"I was at the church talking to a man there about Christianity."

"Of course you were. I told you this morning that I don't want any of that taught in my house."

She stood defiantly before him, hands on her hips. He wasn't sure of how to respond to her, so he said a quick mental prayer.

"My grace is sufficient for thee," he heard in his heart. The same message he had first gotten from the Lord. *Okay*, he thought, *I'll trust Him again.*

"I need to learn more about faith in Jesus. It's important so that I can understand what He wants in my life."

An even angrier look from her told him that this was not moving towards a peaceful resolution.

"You need to leave."

Wow, that didn't take long.

"Wait, please, let me explain—"

"No! I want you out! Until you get this Jesus and Christianity out of your life, don't come back. Your bag is packed and in the hallway. Go now."

This was the most forcefully she had ever spoken to him, even when she'd kicked him out before. He gave her a frustrated yet loving look and picked up his suitcase. As he walked through the door, he gave her one last look.

"I love you."

She continued to glare at him as he shut the door.

The blackness was building around his house and his community.

TWELVE

Kranti had called Arpit, not knowing who else to contact. He was now being shown to a spare room in the pastor's home. He felt awkward and a little ashamed that he had to ask for this help. Arpit knew he was feeling this way and once again assured him that it wasn't a problem.

"I'm not surprised at this at all. You know how our people respond to Christianity."

Kranti nodded. He did know. It was very common back in his country for Christian converts to face great violence.

After settling in for the night, he thought about calling Saachi, but he knew it was too soon. She'd be angry still and expecting him to renounce his new-found faith in Jesus. If there was only some way for him to show her what he'd already learned, but he knew she couldn't understand without being born spiritually. He felt urged to open his Bible and read, so he did.

He flipped open the black leather book and read from a book called Psalms:

> The Lord is my shepherd; I shall not want.
>
> He maketh me to lie down in green pastures: he leadeth me beside the still waters.
>
> He restoreth my soul: he leadeth me in the paths of righteousness for his name's sake.
>
> Yea, though I walk through the valley of the shadow of death, I will fear no evil: for thou art with me; thy rod and thy staff they comfort me.
>
> Thou preparest a table before me in the presence of mine enemies: thou anointest my head with oil; my cup runneth over.
>
> Surely goodness and mercy shall follow me all the days of my life: and I will dwell in the house of the Lord for ever. (Psalm 23:1–6)

He sat and thought about what all of this meant. It seemed that there were many promises in this section of God's Word, all saying that the Lord would provide no matter what he faced. He felt greatly encouraged thinking about this, and he knew he had no need to fear.

It was about an hour early for bed, but he was feeling worn out from the day's events. Lying down, he said a quick prayer, fell into a fitful sleep, and dreamt.

In his dream, he was with Saachi and the boys in their back yard. The boys were playing, just being boys, and he and his wife were laughing at them while some chicken was cooking on the barbecue. As they were enjoying the beautiful sunny day, a black mass formed in the sky. It looked like a storm was coming.

"Rachit, Talat, come inside before the rain comes!" Saachi called to the boys.

Without warning, the blackness descended. As Kranti watched, it completely obscured his vision of his family. As he attempted to move forward to find them, the black smoke came together as if in a vacuum, forming a fearsome demon. The evil being was very large and menacing, carrying multiple weapons and wearing formidable armour. It stood between Kranti and his family and emitted a deep, sinister chuckle.

"You may belong to the King, but these are ours." Its voice was as deep and menacing as its laugh.

Kranti was frozen in place. He hadn't been on his own in a spiritual battle before. He didn't know how to fight this demon and protect his own family at the same time. His enemy recognized his paralyzed state and advanced, raising a massive black blade for a deadly strike. Thunder echoed across the sky's horizon, and a flash of light heralded a bright being, who landed with an equally impressive peal.

"You will *not* harm this human!" Its voice was as powerful as the black creature's, and it was just as imposing. It was adorned in silver armour and bore a majestic blade in its right hand. It stood assertively between the demon and Kranti. It turned to Kranti and placed a hand on his shoulder, which broke his paralysis.

The demon saw a moment of opportunity and struck at the angel, but the being of light raised its shield and blocked the blow.

"Help me push this demon back; use your ability," it commanded Kranti.

Motivated by his words, Kranti concentrated on the psalm he'd read earlier and found the warmth stirring in his chest. The demon noticed Kranti as it continued to fight the angel and it screamed insults and threats at him.

"I'll kill your family! You won't defeat all of us, Evangelist!" The threats were too late, however, as the light began to emanate from within his chest, ever expanding outward until it contacted the black being. The being bellowed in pain as the light pushed it away further and further until it disappeared on the horizon in a puff of black smoke.

Thirteen

Kranti awoke in a cold sweat. The dream had felt so real, and he suddenly saw the angel standing beside his bed. Startled, he again froze in place, like he did in the dream, but the angel touched him.

"Peace," the angel said.

Instantly, Kranti felt peace within his core. The angel then sat in the chair across the room and began to speak.

"I am Ramiel, your protector and assistant. It's good to finally meet you, Evangelist Kranti."

Evangelist Kranti. It was spoken like a title or position. It felt strange but also like it fit.

"I understand the word 'assistant,' but what do you mean by 'protector'?"

"I will come to your aid when you call. It is my duty to protect you from the demons when they become overwhelming."

"Like in the dream when I felt unable to move?"

"Yes, like that. You should also know that the dream was partially real. Your family was never there, but the attack against you was real."

"I can be attacked in my dreams? How do I stop that?"

"You can't, but I can. I was late arriving because I was delayed by another enemy. I won't be late again. I have been ordered to stay by your side."

"Ordered by God?"

"Yes, the Lord himself ordered this."

This was strangely very comforting to him, and he felt as though he could rest again. Ramiel seemed to sense this, and he told Kranti to get some rest, as no harm would threaten him again this night.

Fourteen

S unday morning came and he was well rested but concerned about the previous night's activity. Ramiel was nowhere to be seen, but he'd said he'd been ordered to stay at his side, so he assumed he just couldn't see the angel. He went downstairs and found Arpit in the kitchen with his wife, Ashia, and a fresh pot of coffee.

"Good morning," she said. "Would you like some breakfast or just coffee?"

"Coffee, please." He felt guilty asking for more than this, but eventually the smell of the food was too much and he graciously accepted it.

"We'll be going to the service this morning for ten o'clock. Did you want to ride with us or drive yourself?" Arpit queried.

"I'll drive myself. You're already doing more than enough for me."

"It's no problem, Kranti. Jesus says we should do these things for our brothers and sisters in Him," said Ashia gracefully. She reminded Kranti of Saachi.

Kranti drove to Harmony Christian Fellowship, not knowing what to expect, but he felt that he should be there. He took a seat among the others and listened as they opened the service in prayer and then began singing songs he'd never heard. The words were on the display screens, so he tried to sing along and found that he felt great joy inside of him as he did so.

Looking around the auditorium, he noticed the spiritual condition of the others in attendance and the various colours of the cloaks. The worship leaders had orange as their main or only colour. The pastors were mostly adorned in purple with some silver trimming. There were many other colours present, such as reds and blues as well as yellows and greens. He remembered Arpit explaining that there were many colours and combinations that applied to the various roles of the person.

Realizing that the main speaker had taken the stage and was already reading from scripture, Kranti looked away from the people and focused on the message. The man was reading from the book of Matthew, chapter eighteen, and it seemed to be about forgiveness. Kranti thought about this and wondered, *Who do I need to forgive?* He thought about Saachi but wasn't convinced that she needed to be forgiven, because he understood her position. His sons were innocent, for they were far too young to even understand what was happening. So who then?

"Peter had asked '… *how oft shall my brother sin against me, and I forgive him? till seven times?* Notice he said 'brother,' not 'stranger' and not 'wife.' He said 'brother.'"

Brother? Kranti thought. *I have no brother.* As he pondered this, he seemed to get a message in his mind that this was not just about physical brothers.

So who then counts as my brother?

A spiritual nudge caused him to turn his head and view the auditorium. He then heard a whispering voice say, "All of these are your brothers and sisters now." It was a bit overwhelming, but he began to understand the message. He wasn't sure how to apply it to his life, but he knew what he'd heard.

Fifteen

Kranti was still meditating on the message he'd heard Sunday morning when he arrived at work Monday. His shift started normally and was going as usual, but he did notice some glances from others of his country. He didn't think anything about this until his last coffee break when he went outside to sit with Ben.

"You better come look at this," Ben told him.

"What is it?" Kranti asked.

"Your car."

He walked the remaining distance to his car, and what he saw both angered and sickened him. Scratched into the paint in very large symbols on both sides of the car were hateful sayings. They were in his own language and were very clearly about him becoming a Christian.

"I don't know when this happened. I just noticed it when I came out to my truck," Ben told him.

A bellow of rage escaped Kranti as he viewed the damage and message. He wasn't one to take things like this peacefully. Very quickly his mind tried to sort out who would have done this. He looked at the man in front of him, but he knew that didn't fit. While he was still enraged, a face came to his mind.

Zavian Shah.

"It had to be Zavian. He's the only Indian person who knows I became a Christian!" Kranti spat the words.

"Zavian? How would he know?" Ben asked. Kranti relayed that he had seen and talked to him at Harmony.

"Well, if he's also a Christian, I don't think it's him."

Kranti's rage still showed in his eyes, but he was starting to simmer down a little.

The two men reported what they'd found to the management team. They then covered the sides of the car with cardboard and tape so the messages couldn't be seen.

A lone figure stood out of their sight and laughed.

Sixteen

The rest of the work week went without incident, except for on Friday. Zavian had been told about the car being damaged and was responsible for taking action to prevent this from happening again. He called Kranti to his office to discuss what had happened and what the company had found in their investigation.

"We viewed the cameras outside and we can see some people go to your car. We can see them scratching the letters into the sides of the car, but we can't tell who they were. They were very careful to wear hooded sweaters and masks on their faces as well. We will continue to look into this Kranti, and I'm very sorry that this happened."

Kranti's rage built up again and he let it out.

"Why are you sorry? Did you tell these guys that I'm a Christian now?" It was very accusatory.

"What? No, I didn't tell anyone. How could you think that when I told you I've been keeping my own Christianity a secret?" Now Zavian was angry.

"You are the only one from our country here that knew." Kranti wasn't holding back now.

"I think you need to calm down and think more clearly."

A serious look from Zavian told Kranti that he was pushing his luck. An expletive escaped Kranti's lips before he could stop it.

"Okay, I don't want to do this, but you've gone past the acceptably-angry stage. I'm suspending you for the rest of the shift because you swore at me."

Kranti knew he couldn't argue this point. Others had been suspended for the same thing. Zavian looked at him with compassion.

"You'll be able to come back to work on Monday without a problem."

Kranti was still angry and upset about the suspension as he left the building.

Demonic forces were gathering and celebrating.

SEVENTEEN

Kranti spent the rest of Friday praying and reading the rest of the chapter that the pastor had read on Sunday. He was trying to understand what was happening in his own life, because everything seemed to be falling apart. He couldn't go home because his wife, whom he loved dearly, wasn't willing to listen to him.

He missed his two sons greatly as well and wished he could sit and talk with them. Now he was being attacked by those of his own community at work. He broke down and wept at the overwhelming sadness and hardships he was facing.

"Lord Jesus, I need you now so much. I can't understand what's happening in my life. I have heard that you said your yoke is easy and your burden is light, but I'm having such a hard and heavy time. Please help me, Lord Jesus, please help me!" He had no more words, so he stopped there and just wept in silence for a few more minutes.

He heard the door of Arpit's home open and close and knew that they had come home.

"Kranti?" Ashia called out. "Are you hungry? We brought some butter chicken and saag and some naan bread."

He almost broke down again at the tender care in her voice. It reminded him of better times with Saachi.

"Yes, I'll be right down."

They sat and ate a great meal; it was from the only good Indian restaurant in Dalberton, and it was delicious. Afterwards, Arpit noticed that Kranti was looking like he needed encouragement, so he offered some prayer.

He was surprised at his own response, which was an emphatic "yes." He bowed his head as his host prayed.

"Lord Jesus, we bring to you our brother, Kranti. Lord, you know everything about him and your plans for him. He's being greatly attacked, oh Lord, by the enemy in various ways, and it's becoming a heavy burden for him. Please make the enemy back off we pray, and bring his family back together. We ask that you help his wife to see you as God and Saviour. Help us to help him as well while he's here in our home. In Jesus' mighty name. Amen."

Kranti was grateful for the prayer and concern, and he told them about the chapter he'd been reading. Arpit opened his own Bible and began reading.

Therefore is the kingdom of heaven likened unto a certain king, which would take account of his servants.

And when he had begun to reckon, one was brought unto him, which owed him ten thousand talents.

But forasmuch as he had not to pay, his lord commanded him to be sold, and his wife, and children, and all that he had, and payment to be made.

The servant therefore fell down, and worshipped him, saying, Lord, have patience with me, and I will pay thee all.

Then the lord of that servant was moved with compassion, and loosed him, and forgave him the debt.

But the same servant went out, and found one of his fellowservants, which owed him an hundred pence: and he laid hands on him, and took him by the throat, saying, Pay me that thou owest.

And his fellowservant fell down at his feet, and besought him, saying, Have patience with me, and I will pay thee all.

And he would not: but went and cast him into prison, till he should pay the debt.

So when his fellowservants saw what was done, they were very sorry, and came and told unto their lord all that was done.

Then his lord, after that he had called him, said unto him, O thou wicked servant, I forgave thee all that debt, because thou desiredst me:

Shouldest not thou also have had compassion on thy fellowservant, even as I had pity on thee?

And his lord was wroth, and delivered him to the tormentors, till he should pay all that was due unto him.

So likewise shall my heavenly Father do also unto you, if ye from your hearts forgive not every one his brother their trespasses.(Matthew 18:23–35)

Arpit looked at Kranti and asked him, "What do you think this is trying to teach us?"

Kranti thought before answering. "I believe Jesus is trying to tell us that because we have been forgiven, we also must forgive."

"Exactly. If we have been forgiven so much, we ought to forgive the much smaller offences committed against us, even when they seem to be so serious and harmful to us."

Kranti nodded, beginning to understand. He suddenly realized that he had actually heard a very small voice while talking to Zavian. It had said one word: "Forgive."

Eighteen

Saturday was a very pleasant day for Kranti. He felt much better about his life and situation and enjoyed the day relaxing at the Brar home. He had spent much time also in prayer and studying God's Word.

He went to bed early to be ready for the next day's service, which he was eager to attend. While he was sleeping, though, he heard a sudden *boom* outside that shattered the windows on the front of the house and awoke them all. Kranti quickly got dressed and ran outside to see his car, which had been parked on the street, fully engulfed in flames. Arpit and Ashia came outside and stood beside Kranti while Arpit talked to the police over the phone.

Sirens could be heard in the distance while the car burned, and soon the flashing lights of a firetruck appeared. The truck parked next to the closest hydrant, and firemen connected hoses and quickly put the fire out. The police came soon after and asked whose car it was and if there was any reason for someone to set fire to it.

"You mean someone did this? It wasn't a fault with the car?" Kranti wasn't expecting this.

"Yes, sir, it's very clear to us that this was a Molotov cocktail type of bomb. You see where the gasoline ran off of the roof and down the sides of the car?" The officer pointed to the marks on the car.

"I don't know who would do this," Kranti replied, but he was thinking about the words and symbols that were scratched into the sides of the car.

The fire crew and police were there for two more hours, and the Brars and Kranti spent that time boarding up the broken windows and cleaning up the glass. Afterwards, when the emergency crews had left, they went back to bed to try to be ready for the Sunday service.

The dark demonic beings were dancing in the street around the burnt car.

Nineteen

The service was hard to focus on. Kranti's mind was occupied with the vandalism and fire. He meant to worship, but the stresses were building even though he kept getting the message, "Peace." He could feel that peace within him just a little and knew that Jesus was giving him that to take some of the stress away.

"In John 14:27, Jesus said: '*Peace I leave with you, my peace I give unto you: not as the world giveth, give I unto you. Let not your heart be troubled, neither let it be afraid.*'" The speaker was using this scripture to explain why we shouldn't give in to worry. Kranti was beginning to hear the message but he still wanted to argue about how many bad things had been happening in his life. He was still thinking on these things as he walked out of the service. Another surprise met him in the parking lot as he stepped outside.

Saachi.

She was sitting in her car waiting for him, so he walked over to her. As he got close, she got out of the car. He could see the worry on her face. He opened his arms and she clung to him. She cried silently for a few seconds and then pulled back to look at his face.

"I heard about the bomb. What happened? Why would someone do this? Are you okay?" A million questions in ten seconds—that was Saachi. He cupped her chin in his hand and gave her a reassuring kiss. She relaxed a bit at this and hugged him again and then whispered, "Come home."

His heart leapt at this, and he suddenly realized the full message that was just preached to him. Jesus had told him that He had everything under control, and now He had proven it.

"Thank you, Lord, thank you," he whispered.

They went to the Brars' home and collected Kranti's things. Saachi met them and told them how sorry she was about the damage to their home. Ashia insisted that it wasn't her fault and that the Lord would provide for them.

Twenty

I t was obvious to Kranti that his wife was happy to have him back home. The boys greeted him with cheers and hugs as well, and he knew he was welcome in his own home again. It was a blissful day, and they all spent it enjoying each other's company. Kranti felt the stress melt away.

Saachi and he talked all day about their previous problems. They talked about the changes in Kranti that she noticed and about the scratching and burning of the car. Saachi told him that she'd heard about it from her cousin, who'd been called by a person in the Brars' neighbourhood.

She began to cry again when she mentioned hearing about the bombing. She told him how scared it made her, and that thinking he'd been killed created a fear in her that she'd never known. She felt such an urgency to see him that she got in the car immediately. Her cousin had given her The Brars' address, and she'd driven over there while the Sunday service was on. She saw the burnt ground and grass, and the boarded-up windows. The power of the explosion was evident to her.

Not finding anyone at the home, she could think of no other place to find him but the church. It scared her to go there, as she didn't know what to expect from the people there, and she was worried that someone from their culture or neighbourhood would see her there. In the end, she told him, her need to see him overrode her worries, and she went to find him. He laughed at that, and she playfully punched him for laughing at her.

"Why is that so funny?" she asked.

"It's the message of the day, not you, that's funny," he explained. "It was about worry and how Jesus told His followers not to worry because He would provide for them."

Saachi's eyes widened at this. "Really? That's amazing. It makes me want to know more about Jesus," she admitted, almost ashamedly.

Kranti was overjoyed to hear her say this, but he wanted to proceed carefully.

They spent the rest of the day talking about the Bible and what Kranti had learned about Jesus already. He went into detail about the changes within himself as well, the loss of his desire for alcohol and gambling, and his desire to learn more about his Lord and Saviour. At the end of it all, Saachi looked at him and said that she wanted to know Jesus personally as well.

He told her how he had prayed when he became a Christian, and she bowed her head and spoke. She admitted her need for Jesus and that she believed He was the Son of God, and she asked Him to be her Lord and Saviour. When she raised her head and opened her eyes, she saw her husband in his spiritual armour and gasped in surprise.

"It's okay. I know it's a shock, but you're now able to see the world in the spiritual side of life," he explained to her with a calming hand. "Take a sip of coffee."

She took a sip, and he knew she was back in the physical view of life.

"Wow, that's really weird and really cool," she said in bewilderment.

"I know. I'm still getting used to it," he admitted.

"I feel at peace and full of joy!" she exclaimed.

"Welcome to the family of God." This was all he could say for the joy he felt.

The demonic forces were furious.

Twenty-One

They spent the rest of the day reading Kranti's Bible, talking about what they were reading, and just enjoying a closeness they had never experienced before. Saachi opened up to Kranti about her feelings about him and how he had lived in the past. Seeing her unrestrained honesty, he also shared with her the parts of his past that he had never shared with her before.

In the spiritual view, they talked about his position as an evangelist, as indicated by the silver of his cloak. Saachi examined her own cloak and discovered that hers was a mixture of silver and bronze.

"I see I have evangelism like you, but what does the bronze colour mean?" she asked.

"I don't know. I remember Kathy, who was there when I became a Christian, had an all-bronze cloak. Maybe I should ask Ben about it."

She agreed that they could talk to him about it, but not today. Today was for them to spend together restoring their marriage.

The boys had gone to a friend's house at the end of the street and spent most of the day there. At supper time, they arrived back home, and when they saw their parents sitting close together on the couch, they paused.

"Something is different," the elder, Rachit, stated. "You guys never sit together like this."

Talat, his younger brother, nodded in agreement. "Yeah, are you guys getting a divorce?" Genuine concern sounded in his voice.

The boys' parents both laughed at this and held up hands of reassurance.

"No, no, we are not getting a divorce. We're very happy with each other. Come sit with us and we'll explain why."

The two youngsters sat on the other couch and listened as their parents explained.

"We have become Christians," Saachi told her sons. She let it sink in. "Do you understand?"

The boys wanted to please their parents, but they admitted that they didn't know what this meant.

"It means we've asked Jesus to be our Lord and Saviour," she continued. "He has come into our hearts, and now we are free."

Rachit looked confused. "Free from what, Mother?"

"From sin and judgement and death; free from trying to earn a place in heaven. He paid the price for us, and we just have to accept Him to have salvation."

"So we are no longer Hindu?"

"No, not anymore, but you boys have to choose for yourselves. We can't choose for you."

"Really? I can choose who I want to worship?"

"Yes, but we want you to learn about Jesus so you know who He is."

The boys both said they would listen to stories about Jesus, and they understood that they would go to the church to learn as well.

Dark storms were gathering very quickly in the surrounding neighbourhood.

Twenty-Two

After showing the boys some passages from the Bible about Jesus, Kranti and Saachi prepared for the evening meal. It was the first time in years they had truly enjoyed sitting at the dinner table together.

After dinner, the boys' friends knocked on the front door and wanted them to play at their house again. Kranti and Saachi agreed that they could go but warned them to be back in time for bed. The boys accepted the time limitation and went down the street to enjoy time with their friends.

The happy new Christian couple was enjoying time together cleaning up the kitchen. They were still feeling the joy of salvation and also the joy of being reunited as husband and wife. It was a wonderful time, and the boys soon returned.

As the boys came through the door, Kranti and Saachi heard many voices outside and went to investigate. What they saw caused them great concern.

A large group of their neighbours was gathered in their driveway and on the street in front of their home, and they sounded angry. Kranti came forward and approached the closest people.

"What's going on? Has something happened?"

"We've heard that you have abandoned Hinduism and chosen Christianity! How could you abandon the true religion?"

It became suddenly very clear what was going on, so Kranti switched into the spiritual view. It was a terrifying sight.

He saw many beings of darkness among the people standing in the street. The blackness of them completely blocked out the humans! He looked back at Saachi and whispered "Change into the spiritual view." She quickly did, and he saw the shock on her face and then a look of determination.

The crowd was still yelling at them, and as they grew angrier, the demons began to advance on the two soldiers. Kranti used what little of the scriptures he had learned to fend off the first wave of attackers. Saachi surprised them both by getting in some fatal sword strokes on the smaller enemies. It was becoming clear that they weren't winning against such a large group, and Kranti remembered that he had the ability to shine from his chest.

The brilliant light blasted from his chest, dissipating a massive number of the demonic group. There were still many larger, more powerful fiends moving in on them, though. Saachi instinctively held her hand palm forward, letting go a blast of light directly into the chest of the closest enemy. It screamed and vanished in a cloud of dark smoke.

Things were still very serious when Kranti cried out, "Lord, help us!"

A blinding flash told him that help had arrived in the form of Ramiel. A second angelic being was with the familiar guardian, and Kranti correctly assumed this was his wife's guardian. The two angelic beings destroyed many of the remaining evil host quickly while Kranti and Saachi tried to reason with the human side of this battle.

Their neighbours weren't listening, even without the demonic influence. Many grabbed Kranti and pulled him into the driveway, where they began to pummel him with their fists. Falling to the ground, he called to Saachi, "Get in the house!" The angels also advised her to do so, and she went inside, all the while screaming at the mob to stop.

Dark laughter filled the spiritual side of that scene.

Twenty-Three

"We need the police! Come quickly!" Saachi was on the phone with the 911 operator as she watched in horrified desperation the crowd beating her husband. "I think he's going to die." She sobbed into the phone as the dispatcher tried to calm her down and assure her that police and ambulance services were on the way.

With the sirens sounding in the distance, the crowd kicked the downed man a few more times and then quickly dispersed. Saachi, seeing that they had run away, moved quickly to her husband's side. She gasped at his condition and knelt to attend to his wounds.

He was bleeding from his nose and mouth and had bruises showing on his face already. She could hear that his breathing was strained and saw that the shock of the injuries had left him unconscious. She prayed as the sirens began to draw closer.

"Lord Jesus, please spare my husband. He's seriously hurt, and I need him. Please, in Jesus' name. Amen."

She finished her prayer then because the ambulance was now parked in the street in front of their home. The attendants quickly assessed Kranti's needs and got him into the ambulance. She wanted to ride with him, but the police had arrived and needed a statement from her.

She gave an account of what had taken place, being sure not to identify any of her neighbours. They still had to live amidst these people, and she felt there was a spiritual need here as well. The officer taking her statement seemed to not care about her lack of detail in identifying any of the attackers. She noted that his name was Mitchell and that he seemed to want to be done with this assignment.

After the police left, she went into her home to console the boys. They were scared and shaken, and they began to ask her about their dad.

She tried to calm them, but it was difficult when she wasn't sure herself of Kranti's health.   Suddenly she thought of the Brars and felt peace about calling them for help. She quickly dialled their number and explained to them what had happened. Arpit and Ashia offered to watch the boys for her while she went to see how Kranti was doing. She drove to their home and asked the boys to wait with them while she went to see their dad. They complained at first, until Arpit turned on his gaming console and showed them his games, and Ashia brought recently baked cookies out to them.

Twenty-Four

When Saachi arrived at the hospital, she was told that Kranti had been taken into an operating room. She gasped and grew worried, but they assured her that he was in the best hands possible. Saachi gave the staff information about his health insurance that they hadn't gotten when he arrived, and then she went to wait for news on his condition.

"Mrs. Kholi, your husband has sustained several injuries." A doctor told her after a wait that had felt like a lifetime. "The biggest problem we found was his struggle with breathing. We had to get him on the operating table immediately."

"Is he going to be all right?" Deep concern and worry were on her face.

"He had a puncture to his right lung from a broken rib. We'll need to keep a close eye on him for about a week, but I feel that he should recover with little to no problems."

She thanked the doctor, and a nurse led her to Kranti's room so she could see him for a few minutes. The nurse stayed with her as she examined the bandages and stitches and the breathing machine with the tube that was inserted into his throat. She was careful not to touch him and could only stand close. He was unconscious, so she prayed aloud: "Lord Jesus, Kranti really needs you. He's been hurt so bad. Please heal him and protect him from further harm, because I love him and need him. In Jesus' name. Amen."

"You're a Christian?" The nurse looked at her in surprise.

"Yes. I just became one; my husband is too."

The nurse still had a look of amazement on her face. "I didn't think people from your community could do that."

"Jesus died for everyone, not just White people."

A sound of derision came from the nurse. "Well, visiting hours are finished for the day, so you'll have to come back tomorrow." With that, she made sure Saachi left the room. She then directed her towards the exit and walked away.

Twenty-Five

H aving spent the night with the Brars, for fear of further attack at their home, Saachi awoke the next morning feeling unrested. The first thing she became aware of was a stranger sitting in the chair across from her! After the initial shock, she quickly recognized that it was one of the angels that had assisted them at their home the previous day.

"Hello, Saachi, I am Uriel, your protector." The celestial being spoke directly to her. "I am watching over you, and I have a message for you. Kranti is awake and breathing on his own; he wants to see you."

She was overjoyed to hear this, but she also had questions for this strange creature.

"What is my role in the army of God? I saw that my cloak has silver and bronze evenly mixed in it. What does that mean?"

Uriel looked directly at her.

"Your role is to evangelize with your husband and support him in his role. You are gifted with strength to stand in the battle and to overcome the enemy."

She thought about the battle from the day before and remembered how easily she had defeated some of the demons.

"I experienced that yesterday—the strength, I mean. It was incredible."

"That's what the Lord's blessings feel like—power and confidence in him like you've never experienced. You need to take the boys to see their father now." With this last statement, the angel vanished from her sight.

Twenty-Six

S he found the boys awake and dressed in the living room, listening to Ashia tell them about Jesus. She was amazed at their level of concentration. They were completely captured in what Ashia was saying.

"Jesus told his disciples not to send the little children away. He wants children to come to him." Saachi wasn't sure what part of the Bible she was talking about, but it made the boys smile. They suddenly realized that Saachi was there, and they jumped up and quickly hugged her.

"Mom, can we go see Dad? Please!"

She gave a small laugh and told them to get ready to go to the hospital. While they were getting their shoes on, she turned to Ashia to answer the question on her face.

"I had a visitor in my room this morning."

A look of understanding showed on the other woman's face. "Your guardian."

"Yes. He told me that Kranti is awake, breathing on his own, and wants to see us."

"Praise God!" Great joy was apparent on Ashia's face as she ushered them out the door.

Entering the front door of the hospital, Saachi passed the nurse from the previous night. It seemed she had finished her shift and was going home.

"Good morning," Saachi offered, but she only got a muffled response from the other woman. *I guess she's tired*, Saachi hoped.

They found Kranti's room, and the boys rushed over to him with joyful exclamations. The bed was in the upright position and the breathing machine was gone. He was looking much better than the previous day, and Saachi was greatly surprised at his condition.

"You look so much better! How do you feel?"

"Honestly, I almost feel as if it never happened. Yes, I have some soreness and stiffness, but mostly I feel okay. I had a visitor too."

"Ramiel." She had learned that this was his guardian's name.

"Yes. He told me that I have been healed enough to go home today." A look of joyous surprise from Saachi encouraged him to continue. "He also told me not to be afraid to return home. He said the Lord wants us to work among our neighbours to reach them for Him."

This all made sense to Saachi after what Uriel had told her, and she had a great sense of peace about returning home.

The doctor came in to double check Kranti and was again surprised at his condition. He had been there earlier in the day to take new X-rays and had approved the removal of the breathing machine. He expressed his amazement at his condition once more as he examined the X-rays.

"Mr. Kholi, I can't understand how you have healed so quickly. You were just brought in last night with a punctured lung from a broken rib. Now there is no evidence of those injuries. How is that possible?"

"The Lord has healed me." Kranti's confidence in that statement was evident in his face.

"I don't know about that. I'm a man of science, but I have to admit that this is nothing short of a miracle." He paused for a few seconds to look into the face of his patient. "I see no reason why you can't go home; just keep an eye on how you feel. If you have any reason for concern, don't wait. Come in right away."

Kranti was getting dressed into the fresh clothes that Saachi had brought for him. She was helping him put on his shirt when there was a commotion in the hallway. Screams from nurses and patients echoed down the hallway among cries of "Call 911!" and "He's got a gun!" Saachi looked at Kranti, who motioned to her to stay quiet, hoping the commotion would pass by them.

It didn't. In fact, it came right into his room.

Twenty-Seven

Two men strode purposely into his room, and one of them brought a pistol out of his pocket and pointed it directly at Kranti.

Sammy.

With Sammy was a man Kranti recognized from the confrontation at Murphy's. It was the man who had motioned for the group to leave when the sirens were heard that day. *He must be the leader*, Kranti thought.

"Kill him!" the leader ordered. "This is your final test. If you want your membership, *kill him*!" The man was raging. His face was taut and red, and his glare looked as if it could melt steel.

"Sammy, why?" Kranti asked.

"You keep coming back. The bomb didn't kill you; the mob didn't kill you. You have to die so that this Christian crap stops spreading!"

Two things became very clear to Kranti from this: Sammy was responsible for the car bombing and somehow was involved with the scratches on his car.

His coworker raised the pistol and pointed it at his supposed enemy.

Kranti prayed.

Sammy's hands began to shake. It was clear that he didn't want to kill. His boss became even angrier at him.

"Forget it, kid! You're worthless! I'll take care of this. You're out!"

He snatched the gun away from the younger man, shoving him away as he did. Sammy fell over the chair close to him and was knocked unconscious as his head hit the wall.

The two soldiers shifted into spiritual mode, and they saw several very powerful demons standing with this man. Kranti didn't hesitate but let his light shine as powerfully as he could to weaken the evil beings. Saachi also hit them with her own light, but these were far stronger demons than they had ever encountered. Two sudden heavy thumps announced the arrival of the guardians, and these heavenly warriors began to strike multiple blows on the black beings.

Voices in the hallway indicated that the police had arrived and were trying to assess the situation.

"Mr. Kholi, are you all right?"

It was hard to fight spiritually and respond physically, but Kranti did his best.

"So far, but we have a gun pointed at us!"

A demon charged him but Kranti struck it down with his sword while blocking some fiery darts with his shield.

"*Shut up*!" the biker leader screamed in fury.

"Red? Is that you? I should have known. What are you doing?" the speaker addressed the biker.

"Leave it alone, Al. You know this has to be done. For Jeremy." The last two words were much quieter. In the spiritual side of the conflict, the demons grip seemed to have weakened, and the angels took advantage to eradicate the last of them.

"This isn't the guy who killed him. He's also not that old man!"

There was obviously some unknown history that these two were discussing.

"I don't care! It's been too long, and no one ever found that guy; besides, this guy is a new Christian, and you know they failed us too."

Red's resolve seemed to be waning, although his words were strong. Kranti and Saachi were now standing close together, with the boys behind them and the angels standing in front of them. It seemed that Ramiel and Uriel were indicating that the soldiers should wait, but the couple couldn't understand why.

At that moment, Sammy, who had regained consciousness, grabbed Red's legs and caused him to fall. As he fell, he pulled the trigger and a shot rang out.

"Shots fired!" police yelled, and a canister was lobbed into the room.

Tear gas.

As the smoke filled the small room, all of the occupants began to choke and cough. Seconds later, several officers in masks came into the room and subdued the two bikers. Kranti and Saachi checked the boys but they were unharmed, as were the two parents. The shot from the gun had only gone into the wall without hitting anyone.

Twenty-Eight

Kranti had gotten up early the next morning and was sitting at the kitchen table with a coffee that was slowly getting cold. He was deep in thought, and when Saachi kissed his cheek and greeted him good morning, he didn't respond. She knew what was troubling him, and after making her own coffee she sat next to him.

"You know what you have to do," she said gently.

"Did Uriel tell you?" He looked up from the table that he'd been staring at.

"Yes, and after praying about it, I agree; you need to talk to him. He needs Jesus just as much as we did before we found him."

"Ramiel told me the same thing at the hospital, but I'm having a hard time fighting off my old self. You know how difficult that guy can be—the old me, I mean."

She nodded and gave a light laugh.

"Of course I do, but I also have seen the new Kranti. I believe that the Lord will give you the ability to do this.

He already has given you this ability, and I believe that this is your first act as Evangelist Kranti." She smiled lovingly at him and kissed him.

"Actually, this will be my second act in that role."

She looked quizzically at him.

"You were my first."

She realized that he was right and smiled. At that moment, the phone rang.

"Hello?"

"Hey, Kranti, it's Ben. I just got a call from Officer Mitchell. He wants us to meet him at Murphy's, something to do with Sammy."

Kranti sighed, then laughed out loud.

"Okay, Lord, I'll go." Then he said to Ben, "Please come pick me up. I still don't have another car." Ben agreed to be at his house in ten minutes and Kranti hung up the phone.

"Praise you, Lord. I hear and will obey," he said aloud before preparing to go.

Twenty-Nine

Officer Mitchell was waiting for them, leaning against a classic muscle-car and smoking a cigarette. He was dressed in his own clothing, not a uniform. The man looked completely relaxed, as if this was a normal part of everyday life. He walked up to Ben's truck and greeted the two men. When he spoke, his voice betrayed the conflict going on within him.

"Good morning." He paused and cleared his throat before continuing. "I guess this seems weird, me calling you guys … but I have to talk to some Christians."

A desperate look from the man told Ben something serious was going on.

"No problem, we're here. Let's get some food and talk," said Ben. The distressed man agreed and they found a booth inside to order food and talk privately.

Sipping on his coffee, the officer began to tell them his trouble.

"I want to say, just call me Al. I'm okay with that." He laughed at this as if it were funny somehow. "I'm sorry, I'll try to explain. You see, I did something last night that I haven't done in years, and it's disrupted my whole life."

"What did you do?" Kranti asked.

"I prayed."

Smiles of understanding were threatening to show on the two Christian men's faces, but they held back.

"So what was it that you prayed about?" Ben wanted to know.

"I asked Jesus to come back into my life. I confessed that I had strayed from Him and I wanted to be His again."

They could tell that there was more, but they waited for Al to be ready to talk about whatever that was.

"So what has you so distraught about that?"

Al looked around to make sure no one else was nearby.

"After I said 'Amen,' I opened my eyes and saw my reflection in the mirror. I looked like some ancient warrior! Have I lost my mind?" Now the stress was showing openly on his face.

Ben smiled and suggested they take the coffees outside and get some donuts as well. The three men walked back to where the pickup was parked, and Ben lowered the tailgate for them to sit. Al seemed to be more relaxed away from where others might hear the conversation.

"We've both experienced that, Al. This is what happens when you're born into the army of God," Ben told him. "We all have a position in that army, a role to fulfill."

Questions were evident on Al's face, but he visibly relaxed as well.

"How come I didn't experience this when I was twelve? I prayed the same thing, almost."

"I don't really know. I haven't talked to any children about becoming a Christian. Maybe it's different for them, or maybe you weren't sincere back then."

"I'll have to think about that. It's been a long time, almost twenty years, since I first prayed to Jesus."

"It was a big shock for me too. I also felt like I was going crazy," Kranti added.

"So how does it work? Because I had a hard time turning it off, and now I can't turn it back on."

"Switching between views is tricky at first. We use food to switch out of what we call the 'spiritual view.'" Ben motioned towards the donuts and coffees.

They continued discussing how to switch between views for another fifteen minutes, and when Al had a good understanding of it, he grew sombre.

"There's something I should explain to you about Red and myself." He paused, and it was clear that this was a difficult subject for him. "Red and I grew up together.

We met when we started school, and we spent everyday together." Another pause as he gathered his emotions. "Jeremy Parker started at our school in grade 5, and we both instantly liked him. We became three peas in a pod, travelling to and from school together. We spent every minute with each other; this is how we were for two years."

He took a drink from his coffee to steel his nerves.

"Jeremy was from a Christian home and had invited us to go to church with him. We went to the youth nights and Sunday services many times with his family. Eventually, Red and I answered the altar call at one of the youth nights.

"That night Red and I were feeling peace and joy like we had never known. Jeremy was overjoyed that we had accepted Jesus for our own Lord and Saviour. After the service, we got on our bikes and began the short ride to our homes. We all lived close to each other and were just up the street from our homes. Jeremy had been a little behind us, and we looked back to see where he was. I guess the chain had come off again and he was leaning over and putting it back on the front gear. He didn't even seem to hear the car."

He had to stop for a few minutes as he got to the most traumatic part to tell. Breathing deeply, he looked directly at the two men in front of him.

"We watched as the driver drove directly into Jeremy. The man never even slowed down; he just kept on driving. I'll never forget that day or that scene, and neither will Red."

THIRTY

B en and Kranti weren't sure how to respond to such a horrifying tale.

"I believe that Jeremy was brought into your life for the purpose of showing Jesus to you and Red," Ben suggested. "Maybe that was the main goal the Lord had for him. Jeremy did his job well, so it was time for him to go be with the Lord." He then recounted his own loss and how Harold had experienced the exact same loss decades earlier, just so he could tell him of that loss and Ben could find Jesus.

"Wow, that's incredible. But why does God use the most horrible experiences? Why did He allow us to go through something so awful? Red and I had just chosen to follow Jesus, so there was no need for it."

"For some of us, we don't listen until something horrible happens. It's the only thing that got my attention."

"What happened to Jeremy wasn't the Lord's doing," Kranti stated. "That was demonic influence over the driver; it had nothing to do with God."

"I agree with Kranti. There is a lot more demonic influence in the world than most realize."

"Demons? I'm not sure how to handle that."

"We've all been given different abilities spiritually, and they are exactly what each of us needs to fight off these enemies. Let's switch back into the spiritual view. I want to show you something."

They focused and the world shifted as their view of it changed. Al was again shocked at the difference, but he began to curiously examine this new perspective.

"We all seem to look the same, except that the cloaks on our backs are different colours. Mine's a deep blue, like sapphire mixed with a medium blue. What does that mean?"

"Both blues refer to law and authority, and it indicates that your position is Protector, which doesn't sound so exciting, I know."

Al gave a chuckle.

"No, it's pretty accurate. 'Serve and Protect,' you know? I also think of the force as helping others, looking out for those who can't look out for themselves." The experienced officer smiled grimly. "I know who I need to help first."

"Red," Kranti expressed.

"Yes. I just hope I'll know what to say to help him find the Lord."

"I'm confident that you will."

EPILOGUE

The Kholi family had been back in their home for about a month. They had initially been worried about more problems from the neighbours or the biker group. After some serious heartfelt prayer, Kranti and Saachi had gotten the same message from God: "*Have not I commanded thee? Be strong and of a good courage; be not afraid, neither be thou dismayed: for the LORD thy God is with thee withersoever thou goest*" (Joshua 1:9).

With this encouragement, they moved back into their home with confidence. They removed the symbols of Hinduism that were displayed at their house and even hung a small cross above the garage door. Within two weeks, a few of the neighbours had come to ask them about Christianity. After this, they posted a sign below the cross that said:

All Welcome
Bible Study: Saturday 7:00 p.m.
Questions about Jesus: Anytime

WARRIOR OF LIGHT

Ben Parsons' grief over tragedy has brought him to a
dead-end. Then a wrong-number call shows him the
spiritual side of life and that there is another road to take.

Coming Soon

SERVANT OF LIGHT